The Jeweled Moon

Daniel Tyler-Ray

Omecronon

ISBN 978-9187713071

The Jeweled Moon

The cold, jeweled moon, blistered against my feet as I walked up to Mary's mansion; or should I say home. It hadn't been a happy time lately and I wasn't impressed by her 4 flight under storage room where she kept her cloudy secrets just as if she was Swedish or something equally distasteful. Bird watching was the name of the game and if you know the name of the game birds tend to fly differently depending on the season, so consider the birds dear Mary and let me in.

She didn't let me in; the clouds told me so. There's a hippo living in all of us and if you find this to be a strange story then by all means read

Boris Vian or get a new taylor. The furry clouds were just that; furry. Not fluffy as some US comedian gladly would have them.

What's wrong with people anyway? Why can't they appreciate something novel? Why does everything has to go on repeat? Oh! I forgot! It's all about oil. Alladin's lamp doesn't seem all that important to me; all it tells is lies anyway. Tales of lies and deception; the deception of mankind? Maybe! Anyway Vian is in fashion again. Haven't seen him around for a very long time. I guess the world is going to end because we're afraid of novelties (and I'm not talking about Lou Reed's new age here – that guy is much overrated regardless of what Rushdie thinks.)

Mary, mother of all who do not know what it's like to have a child. You will surely look away. Sometimes I believe that it was Thomas who was right. A twin star has to have a twin brother and I mourn for India; this poor and tormented country all because of a nation the language of which I tend to use when writing.

Mary, mother of all who does not know what it's like to have a child. I neither raped nor revered you. I know for a fact that I was not born in sin; no man or woman is born in sin. Hence I can enjoy the gospels but I cannot believe. Once a pope was raped I believe. But then of course it's easy to ask for forgiveness; like Pasteur. How does the tune go? We have some kitchen delivery. Oh my! Does that one has to go on repeat too before some of those who don't understand much starts to think. I was dreaming of creating poetry that made up a framework for thought but it fell dead from the press to paraphrase the Empiricist David Hume. People seem afraid of thinking whereas I find it to be a virtue; that is one explanation why people are afraid of the new; even in literature. Set your mind free for Christ's sake, and feed your mind.

Is it hard to be human? People say so but what they forget is the Kirkegardian suicide; dying from happiness. The middle path, preached by so many, seems to be the safest way to go. I hope that I'm not disturbing people now and make them ill at ease. It was never my intention; only serious thoughts needs serious language. A death like Kirkegaard wrote would be something. Kirkegaard, the Dane, also wrote somewhere (I don't recall where) that when the world ends it will be like people sitting in a theatre watching a comedy not noticing that the theatre is in flames.

It is getting late and my lamp flickers. I bid you a humble au révoir.

Cynical Like a Buddha and the Smile of Mona Lisa

"Sure," the Jewish Madame said when the Buddhist stayed at the Savoy hotel. I have to admit that she had a point but the leaders of men as some British guy sang, aren't very keen on living modestly. I like the Jewish Madame; I owe her a lot. Maybe my life. Or maybe my life had looked differently if I wasn't so damn stubborn.

I could never be a monk; lack the discipline.

"I believe in God because I don't believe in God"

The thing written above is a good example of Thai humour. Toying with logical negations was always correct and one wonders if the smile of Mona Lisa isn't an ironic one and not a mystic one.

If so, the smile of Mona Lisa can be Buddhist in nature. The student asks "Who am I?" The master monk answers "Look inside and you might find it." Of course this never happens and the monk knows it; hence the smile.

The Buddha must have had a great time putting logical negations in front of most things in Hinduism. It's not just that he rejected the caste system, it's perhaps more than that. The present day Buddha has turned into Ronald MacDonald and are we to celebrate this? What lies behind the ironic smile of the monk? What lies behind the smile of Mona Lisa? Is it possible that there was a connection between the painter and the east? Considering the smile this is not farfetched it seems to me.

What was in Thomas Mann's head when he wrote *Der Zauberberg?* Oh! He was bisexual; everyone knows that. But what does Switzerland, this post card-country, has to do with anything? It's indeed a pity that many famous people are more known for their lifestye than their work. I could bounce on Beyoncé anytime; it's just that I'm not as rich as that. Does she smile? Is it real or hidden behind 100 layers in Photoshop?

NO!! I tell you!!! Atlantis won't rise. Francis Bacon was Francis Bacon and Shakespeare was another character. To be is not! To be in becoming is everything!! Thus both Shakespeare and Bacon were wrong. But then again; the world was smaller when they lived.

Yesterday I sat on a bus and I had a mother in front of me with a baby sitting in a baby carriage. Maybe it was to distract or entertain; I don't know; but all of a sudden the mother handed her smartphone to the small child to show her some pictures. When she'd done that I said in English "So this is Armageddon. Do you really want it to end…now?" Of course the mother didn't seem to notice me.

I'm not anti much but I don't want our children to grow up in a 3D graphical environment where what they do have repercussions somewhere else on the planet.

I'm ashamed of my blue eyes and a singer I sometimes listen to has a one-liner saying "don't let the blue eyes fool you". Tomorrow Elvis Presley's Blue Suede Shoes will be on sale for 50 cents.

It's a thin line between irony and cynicism.

Here's looking at you Ronald.

Diamonds, Earrings and Mysterious Matters

The title of this piece is merely to lead you into thinking something special will come but I'd hesitate to say so. After all this talk about religion and serious matters it's, I believe, high time to get our heads into the clouds only not to find anything there in that fluffy substance (that dreams are made of). Prince couldn't have done it better himself but that was diamonds and pearls... oh! Classic!!

I've often wondered about languages. The Latin languages seem very rash to me whereas the Germanic languages don't share that characteristic. On the contrary they seem to fool one another; deceive one another. I wonder which is the most deceiving language of German and Swedish. I really can't tell. Dutch seems more neutral in that respect but then the Dutch are peace lovers whereas the other Germanic countries seem to want to create trouble everywhere. Take Siemens as a brilliant example of a fatal failure. Get my drift? Fukoshima mon amour!

In 2011 Italy got credits for finding particles travelling faster than the speed of light which is impossible in current day Physics. It was a collaboration between CERN in Switzerland and Italian universities. This was a breakthrough and the experiments were set on repeat with similar results. Science never ends almost per definition and there might come a time when Einstein is outdated but as for the experiments in Europe in 2011 I bet that they used some drunk PhD student in doing the experiments. Or maybe someone who was high on drugs. This little experiment seem to be apart in a chain of events that deserve a treatise of their own as they are very complex in nature and pertain to a great deal of society (but it seems that Switzerland and Italy have more in common than Switzerland and other Germanic countries).

I'd better quit now before I lend myself to too much speculation; they say it's not good.

A Crescent yet to Grasp

Mary may not have given birth but thy beauty, oh crescent, has given birth to me in my becoming. It's ripe but I'm not 30 and there's no mountain to step down from. Moreover the cup isn't full. It's not the new Atlantis; it's still the old world tormenting us. We live in a protected environment with Osmos pressure, fragile as a feather of an adjacent bird as I stand by my window trying to trace the motion of birds in the sky. Maybe there will be a Califonia earthquake. It will surely mean the world for Califonia but what will it mean for the world? What did they ever give us this people without history?

What makes up the beauty of the crescent so in tune with my becoming? It's feather light and both faint and distinct. A contradiction? Surely not! Faint as in distant and distinct as in vision. I too, am feather light but my task is to grasp the crescent. The aim of man is to grasp the crescent while it's there; the marble told me. If there is hope? Oh yeah! Once a month a crescent is born which is not to say it's a moon festival. Half a lifetime ago I was at Koh Pangan. Now it's all exploited. Back then people were poor and humble fishermen. John Lennon wanted to be a fisherman if he had to do it again. I don't envy him.

Just watching the crescent purifies the mind for sure. It speaks of becoming and imputes it in us.

I say nothing of a wounded earth. I say nothing about time being twisted. All I ever wanted for myself was a space in which to breathe because I realized at an early age that the nation where I reside is not really a democracy and moreover it's not a good one. The Swedish model is based on terror; it's quite similar to the American dream in a way. Don't buy that crap, please. You're better off. Sweden is a duck farm where everyone is watching everyone and "every move you make" as the Geordie sang is monitored daily. Freedom and justice are just buzzwords. Never mind the buzzwords or Santa will get you.

Then all of a sudden two earrings colliding. My girlfriend must have imploded. Maybe she couldn't take the competition. Oh well! Better throw her away and get a new one.

Lightening up the Ingmar Bergman syndrome - A Different Approach to Playing Chess

Knight: Here's looking at you kid.

Death: What do you mean? Who are you; Bogart?

Knight: Oh no. I'm just an average guy but I do have somewhat of a crush on someone.

Death: Crush? What's that?

Knight: It's complicated. You wouldn't understand. But I fancy you.

Death: Huh?

Knight: Never mind. Let's continue playing.

Death: Excuse me but you've disturbed my circles.

Knight: Chess.

Death: Oh my!

Knight: What do you think? It's not child's play you know.

Death: I know, I know. We all have our crosses to bare. You're a knight right?

Knight: You can call it that but I have a subscription for the journal of Consciousness. The complete issues.

Death: The journal of ... what?

Knight: Consciousness studies.

Death: Hmm. Sounds scary.

Knight: Calm down will you.

Death: Can I ask for your expertise, please?

Knight: Of course! Go ahead.

Death: You're a knight, right but then who am I?

Knight: Not sure. Haven't reached that stage yet. Anyway, I have a clown to consider. Can we continue the game.

Death: I feel shaky.

Knight: That would be scientifically adequate here, I suppose.

Death: Oh my! What can I do?

Knight: Chess mate! I win. Sorry.

Death: Oh my! I didn't expect this. It's not in the script.

Knight: Forget about scripts. Don't you have any imagination?

Death: Imagination? What's that?

Knight: It's a property of consciousness.

Death: Seems handy. How do I get it?

Knight: An annual subscription for a magazine on consciousness comes with a beautiful life insurance. If you get it from me, that is.

Death: Life … life … Rings a bell somehow.

Knight: In that case I might tempt you to find out more.

Death: Oh yeah!

Knight: My sincere apologies for winning the game but as compensation you can get 50% off the insurance.

Death: Is there any catch.

Knight: I have two horse nearby. You have to ride one of them.

Death: Horses. They are ... they are ...

Knight: Living yeah.

Death: Oh my. How do I mount one then.

Knight: It's included in the insurance letter. Don't worry.

Death: Thank you so much, sir knight. This is the best thing that ever happened to me. I've always loathed this role. It's all black and white and I'd like to see colour some day.

Knight: Look over there. It's sunset. Beautiful.

Death: Where?

Knight: We better mount the horses. You'll have a better view then.

Then the knight and death rides happily through a Swedish desert towards the sun and a place where smoking is prohibited.

16

One day it was in the daily news. The story ran 2 pages with pictures. It was about a girl who had cut her arms for years. It was all over the pages with pictures. The story of her tragedy went on in the form of an interview and she said that she had found comfort in her new boyfriend and that had made her quit. A month passed and then the entire country had young girls cutting their arms with razorblades. The tragedy was that it was too much to handle for the hospitals.

Anthropology is a bitch at times. Luckily Philosophers didn't come up with the synergy concept which is known as "dynamic effect" in the media. A dynamic effect can be a great deal but the very notion of a dynamic surely sounds like a lasting sales argument. Never mind the young ones, here are the ones who prefer dogs to people.

As a former worker in the Kinnevik group I'm well aware of the fact that they preferably want everyone to work on a commission and it shouldn't be more than 1 pound per hour. That's how cynical they are. I never regret quitting that job.

I've been in the board of a magazine myself once. I was one of the favourites in the board and I received very versatile tasks to do. Those were interesting times and the magazine in question was a very friendly one, although with a rather strange name. With my academic background I was constantly corrected. In the academy you write in passive form I was told, whereas in journalism you write in active form. I enjoyed my journalist time but I miles prefer the academic jargon to the journalist one. Why? Because in the academy nothing is proven and there always has to be a degree of uncertainty – hence the passive form (for example).

The drawback of the academy is when words are picked up and overused. One example is synergy. Also the very word science has been a victim for inflation. Here it's called "literature science". Why? Do they run stats on how many times the letter "T" is used in Homer? Oh my, have we gone mad?

Somebody had a Body to go With the Beer

The queen is dead boys and stark is the word not to be forgotten; my memory escapes me not having been north of the polar circle. There, if anywhere, the water is alive with penguin soul, sandy desolate mermaids who can't sing much because of the weather; it's simply not hot enough for Homer's mast.

If anyone has a body to go with the beer then I don't mean just any Mac; I mean the real thing; a talisman too hot to handle; a seal; a bond (not like in the movies though). I met an Irish boatman and I asked him if he was really into what he was into doing. He responded in a stark way. Stout? Maybe too proud to be stabbed by

Monthy Python who the French don't seem to fancy much. So you've seen la tour Eiffel? That don't impress me much and neither Does the Librarie Nationale de France where there are no books to be seen. The French pay too much attention to modern technology. A computer in French is called ordinateur. That's what it's supposed to do or used to if Aristotle was right but alas he wasn't. The law of the excluded third is long since superseeded. I believe it was Oscar Wilde who did it in the modern world; if modern is appropriate to Wilde. Wilde might be appropriate to Guy Debord (and now everyone with an interest in Sociology faints – their icon par excellence).

Now I walk on the party-strewn pavements of yesterday remembering only the painted faces of time machine women masquerading like for the last time. The island storms are put to rest and the cool bejeweled moon smiles in a cold and solemn fashion as it's full and I'm starving for sincerity in a postmodern crescendo of dúrété and lourdesse. Damn!

Howdy, said the bat to the elementary particle. Is there anyone in space who can still recall what it's like to learn what we learnt at school? I shouldn't come on too pretentious if not for inviting my reader, enticing my reader, challenging my reader to think outside the box as it's often called (we live by metaphors like that). Oh my! What have I done? Sown a seed? I hope and pray that yes, one day, a new Phoenix will rise and we will be one here in Pangea. Brittle tears subside with the rain that strew the pavement and I seek myself indoors. I'm a lucky bitch 'cause I can go indoors ...

I stand by the window watching the bejeweled moon and try to detect its language. Every star has a language, even those who are 17 times more heavy than the entire Milky Way. How come they're not visible? Do we believe in astronomy or? Is Kant outdated? Are we living in an age of forgery? I wouldn't like to think so but then again ...

It's Zen and the art of forgery. Calling a spade a spade is somehow nonsensical.

Non Enchantment

His lover had left him a note. It wasn't very elaborate but quite brief. He read it and couldn't believe it. He read it again and again. He still couldn't believe it. Everything had been fine between them up to a certain point. They had an argument, but he felt like it was just one of those things. It was going to pass. They had been lovers for a year and everything seemed stable. It seemed as if they were destined to continue. He was very much in love and so was she; or at least up to this point. This sudden change made him uncomfortable, to say the least. The only thing that was written was that she had found another man and was leaving him.

This came from out of the blue. A couple of days earlier they had met over a nice dinner and everything had been grand. They had even made love. How long had she had this other man? The letter didn't say. A lot of questions went through his mind. It wasn't an ordinary train of thoughts; there were a great deal of different things that sprung up. He went through – or tried to go through – all that had happened between them recently but he couldn't find anything that could have caused this except for the argument they had a week ago. The argument was rather silly. It was like one of those arguments that couples that have been married for decades have. It was not a big deal and nothing that could possibly trigger this. In a state of sudden haziness he dropped the note on the table and lied down on the bed.

What could he do? Contact her, of course. Phone her up and ask her to expand on it. But the fact that she had sent him a letter and hadn't told him in person, eye to eye, made him hesitant. It didn't seem very courageous of her not to tell him to his face. Maybe she didn't want to talk to him. But he felt that the letter was so short that a great deal of things were left out. She had found another man. Well, why had she looked for one in the first place? They were doing fine together and there were no signs that their relationship would end. So what to do? He had to phone her but there was a risk that she wouldn't answer, considering the phrasing of the short letter which was pretty cool and sharp. How could she do it? Who was she to end it anyway? They were two to decide on such a thing and he didn't want to let go. But he supposed that he had to. He only had to find out why. The whole thing hurt him. He could feel it to his bone.

Whiplash

Who was he to be abandoned like this? What had he done to deserve it?

Night came like a black cloth and he couldn't get any rest. His mood was low and he was almost frantic and sleep simply didn't come to him. He kept thinking about his lost girlfriend and what they had experienced together in the past. How much they had in common. How much they had shared over this year they had been together.

How they had laughed together; how they had cried together. It had been a very deep relationship and thinking about it he felt a sudden ache in his heart; it was very real. He was low; he felt ill. He didn't know what to do about it. It was all because of her. She. She is.

Night continued and no sleep. His mood altered between distress and a sense of being terribly, terribly hurt. He couldn't understand. His mind lingered in the past; in the past that had seemed so fine.

Morning came and the phone rang. It was Michael.

-How are you?

-I'm ok. And you?

-Fine. I was just wandering if you need anything. Do you need to borrow money or something?

-Well. Things are pretty scarce but I think I'll manage. Thanks.

-No problem. I'm here if you need anything. You know that.

-Yes I do. You're so kind. A real friend.

-Are you sure you're ok?

-Yes. Why?

-You sound a little gloomy.

-Oh. It's just temporary. I've had a bad morning

-Oh well. If you need me I'm here.

-No problem. See you then.

-Yes. Bye.

-Bye.

So they hang up. He didn't feel the need to tell Michael about his girlfriend. Michael was an old and very dear friend but the time was not right. He needed to sort matters out with the lady first. Money. Yes. It was true he didn't have much. He had lost his job three months ago and he'd had a hard time getting a new one. He had applied for a great deal of jobs but not a single interview. He did have rather good record. He had been in insurance. Not the best business to be in but he had managed quite well. But he was sacked because of the recession. They had told him they needed to make some priorities and so he had to go. He became unemployed instantly. Financially this was a blow. He was temporarily not connected to any union and at present hew didn't have much to live by. His girlfriend, or former girlfriend had a very good position with a publishing house. She was doing quite well. They were both ex-academics. The difference between them was that the woman had picked the right classes and he hadn't. So he was stuck with insurance, a job he didn't feel very comfortable with but had grown used to over the years. But now he was unemployed, and that was a big drawback for him. If it went on for much longer he would be in great danger of losing what he had; all for financial reasons. God how he detested the economic circus he and everyone else were woven into. But there was no way of escaping it. Everyone has to play along.

How long was he going to wait before he called her? He didn't know but considering it was Saturday he'd better wait until noon. It was ten o'clock so he had to wait for an hour and a half or so but he didn't know if he disliked it. There was something about the entire idea of phoning her that seemed repellent to him but at the same time he knew he had to. His heart told him so. Bloody heart!

Love Letter from Abundant Waters

The opaque sky,

Is all in tears tonight.

Rainy women,

Brings to mind

My rainy eyes

When I carried my love

Maya – un encore;

Only once more,

Only one more time.

World is ascending,

And the green eyes of mine,

Are jaded by the midnight rain,

I often liked.

In hindsight,

Things always seem different.

My sadness bleeds through

As I miss you.

All I ever loved for real,

Has been tranquilized.

Hue, Saturation, Brightness;

It's in the eye of the beholder,

And I'm dirtier than thou.

It's ironic,

For the women know who I am,

Whereas the men who have known me,

Never noticed that I'm older now.

The reality generators,

Tend to malfunction for some;

And it's a shame,

That these people,

Are considered weak.

It takes strength and courage,

To be weak,

In a special case,

Of an artificial paradise.

It is we who are the angels of light;

Let us not forget that.

Now when I've Bored You

Now when I've bored you with a poem (I know it's not in fashion) then I believe it's time to wrap it up. Did I ever touch upon the weather? What does Mary has to do with anything. Ama la natura! I'm a latin guy you know, despite the name I go by. Moreover I should be thankful because I have a roof over my head in 2014 and a computer since they've superseded the pen in writing stuff like this. For better or worse I'm hesitant to say. There's so much crap out there for this little piece to "compete" with and I hope to do better next time (there WILL be a next time so remember me please – I have a novel in the works). Christ how I loathe writing about myself. There are too many of those out there already.

I don't and won't thank god for my daily bread but I send my gratitude to the people who've worked to keep my standards of living high enough to pen this down and while I'm at it I'd like to encourage you to do the same. You and me are nothing if not for the myriad creatures as Lao puts it (not sure if he'd appreciated my use of his concept here though). Yeah, I'm well read but hey, it's still Zen and the art of refinery or forgery (depending on how you look at it). We live in a hyper capitalist society and even a book like this must be sold at ultra speed. Fortunately I'm not a vendor but that doesn't mean I'm free. Freedom is just one of those buzzwords and as such overused.

It's running late on planet earth and my lamp flickers once more. I need to stay awake though; remain awake until the North Pole meets the south and what remains is ridiculous. In metropolis there is no space to breathe and as for the clinic, Omecron, I say a decisive "no". Nobody would find that livable; nobody. Omecron was or is the name of a piece of dystopia yet to finish and as for dystopia... well... I figured out that we live in it daily. Chins up anyway dear reader because It's not the end of the world, it's only the end of humanity; the end of joy, happiness and virtue.

Since Omecron is a fact there is no need for me to finish that manuscript; it will probably fall dead from the press. My lamp has flickered enough and my eyes are weary from vision. I have no nice twist to end this piece so I just say that it's the final curtain.